② Battering Rams

The electrifying serial continues ...

It all began like this.

When Dawn's dad and Rory's mum got married, Dawn and Rory became step-sister and brother. That was pretty bad.

But what happened next was even worse. Rory's pet worms turned into horrible bone-sucking slobberers. They sucked a magpie dry. And a possum.

Then Dawn and Rory found their parents' wrecked car with its blood-stained seats. That's when they really started to panic.

Was it the slobberers?

Are Dawn and Rory next on the menu?

Read on. *Battering Rams* will suck you in deeper.

Wicked!

(2) Battering Rams

Morris Gleitzman and Paul Jennings

PUFFIN BOOKS

PUFFIN BOOKS

Published by the Penguin Group
Penguin Books Ltd, 27 Wrights Lane, London W8 5TZ, England
Penguin Putnam Inc., 375 Hudson Street, New York, New York 10014, USA
Penguin Books Australia Ltd, Ringwood, Victoria, Australia
Penguin Books Canada Ltd, 10 Alcorn Avenue, Toronto, Ontario, Canada M4V 3B2
Penguin Books (NZ) Ltd, 182–190 Wairau Road, Auckland 10, New Zealand

Penguin Books Ltd, Registered Offices: Harmondsworth, Middlesex, England

First published in Australia by Penguin Books Australia 1997
Published in Great Britain in Puffin Books 1998
5 7 9 10 8 6 4

Copyright © Greenleaves Pty Ltd and Creative Input Pty Ltd, 1997
All rights reserved

Set in Cheltenham

Made and printed in England by Clays Ltd, St Ives plc

British Library Cataloguing in Publication Data
A CIP catalogue record for this book is available from the British Library

ISBN 0–140–38991–1

ONE

It **was night.** I was miles from home in a lonely wrecker's yard. Next to me was a bus with the only remaining part of my mother in it. Giant slobbering worms were straining at the battered yard gate, desperate to suck out my bones.

And what was it that made me run blindly into the darkness in terror?

A dog.

Dawn the chicken, that's what Rory would have called me. Well he'd have been wrong.

The dog was a killer. It had a savage snarl and huge teeth. Its saliva had bubbles in it, not from eating soap, from being so vicious.

1

DAWN

When it charged at me with its huge jagged mouth wide open, I ran.

Scary broken-down farm equipment loomed out of the darkness. I crashed into something, scraping my arm on rusty metal. I kept running until I tripped and sprawled painfully in the dirt. I scrambled up, heart thumping, expecting to see dog-food-stained teeth coming for my throat at any second.

But the dog was over by the gate, leaping up at the slithering tongues of the giant worms. My heart slowed down to very fast. The dog hadn't been going for me, it had been going for the slobberers.

There was enough moonlight for me to see my hands trembling with relief.

I heard feet scampering towards me.

'Rory,' I tried to yell, but all that came out of my parched throat was a croak.

I strained to see if it was Rory. He was about as hopeless a step-brother as you could get, but at that moment I really wanted it to be him.

It wasn't. It was a sheep.

We looked at each other, startled. Then the sheep grinned.

I blinked. Was I imagining it? Had terror scrambled my brain? Sheep didn't grin.

Get real, I told myself. It's just got wind.

A screech of twisting metal rang out across the yard and the sheep bolted. I turned towards the sound. The gate was slowly groaning inwards. Then it fell.

A sea of slobberers poured in.

I stood frozen with terror. I knew they'd been growing, but I was shocked to see how big they were. Most of them were fatter than the sheep. In the moonlight they looked like angry, slurping vacuum cleaners without the wheels.

I didn't want to see what they did to the dog, but I was too slow turning away. The horrible image burned into my brain and I felt sick. No dog deserved that, not even a vicious one. No step-brother did either.

'Rory,' I tried to scream, but my vocal cords were in shock and all I could do was squeak.

I looked frantically over at where I'd last seen him. That part of the yard was alive with slobberers. Green eyes glinting. Wet tongues sliming.

A sob forced its way out of my throat.

The slobberers started moving towards me.

As I turned and began running again, I heard other running feet nearby.

Thank God. Rory was okay.

I sprinted in the same direction. Soon I could see the shape of a figure up ahead. I tried to yell but I had no breath.

Neither did the running figure. He was wheezing and gasping. His white hair was flopping. His pot belly was rising and falling with each step.

My guts fell too. It wasn't Rory. It was the old caretaker.

'Wait,' I yelled, sucking in air. 'Rory's back there. You've got to help.'

The caretaker lumbered on. I forced my legs to go faster and caught him at his car door as he fumbled with his keys.

'Please,' I gasped. 'Please help.'

He turned, saw me, and gave a yell.

'Arghhh.'

I'd never had an adult yell at me in fear before, and for a couple of seconds I didn't know what to say.

Then I did. 'You're our only hope,' I pleaded. 'My mum's dead, and Rory's dad's nicked off, and my dad and Rory's mum have had an accident on their honeymoon and disappeared and they could be dead too.'

Panting, I waited for him to digest this and then get some really high-powered slobberer-strength guns out of his boot.

Instead he glared at me.

'I know you're not real,' he said, and blew a raspberry at me.

I was stunned. But I didn't have time to be stunned

4

for long. 'I *am* real,' I said, and kicked him in the ankle to prove it.

He winced and rubbed his ankle with his other foot.

'That wasn't real either,' he said, scowling. 'Lousy doctor. What's the point of heart pills if they make you see stuff and get palpitations.'

He hurled a bottle of tablets into the darkness. Then he got into his car, slammed the door and started the engine.

'Wait,' I begged. 'We're just two kids. Probably only one now.'

The caretaker spun his tyres in the dirt and the car took off, flattening a second rusty iron gate and skidding over it in a cloud of tyre smoke.

As I watched his rear lights getting smaller in the darkness, I suddenly felt small too. And very alone. Suddenly I wanted Mum and Dad, both of them, with their arms round me and their soft voices in my ears. I crouched in the dirt and squeezed my eyes tight so the tears wouldn't sting so much.

At first I thought the sound of mucus bubbling was me crying. Then I opened my eyes and saw it wasn't.

A slobberer, the biggest of the lot, was writhing slowly about a car's length away from me. Its green eyes were fixed on mine and I could see the blue veins in its slithering, hungry tongue.

DAWN

I screamed.

The slobberer's eyes glowed brighter and it slimed towards me like a big vinyl bag on a luggage carousel with all its shampoo and moisturiser oozing out.

I stepped back and scraped my leg on something. A steel fence post sticking out of a pile of scrap. I grabbed it and raised it above my head and closed my eyes and swung it down onto the slobberer with all my strength.

It was a shock.

I expected a squish and what I got was a thunk. The slobberer was solid muscle. The fence post vibrated and so did my hands and arms and shoulders and major internal organs.

I opened my eyes.

The fence post was bent.

The slobberer was slithering backwards. Then it stopped, shuddered and suddenly went sloppy like liver when you cut open the plastic bag.

I didn't take my eyes off it.

After a bit I chucked a metal bolt at it. The bolt sort of sunk in. The slobberer didn't move. Its eyes were grey.

I peered over at the other side of the yard. The rusty hulk of the bus was completely surrounded by slurping, tongue-waving slobberers.

Mum's bus.

Suddenly my fingers weren't numb any more. Blood tingled through my body. I thought of Dad, my only remaining parent, who was probably next on the slobberers' menu. One scrawny kid and a dog wouldn't keep them going for long.

I gripped my fence post and walked slowly towards the slobberers.

Okay, there were heaps of them. Okay, there was only one of me.

But now I was as angry as they were.

TWO

As the slobberers poured into the wrecker's yard, I slammed the door in a panic and stared out of the bus window with wide, terrified eyes. They were still sucking their way after me – looking for a meal. Ever since I'd cut my hand on the fence trying to escape them, they'd followed the bloody trail I'd left behind me.

A few metres from the bus they suddenly stopped. They sniffed and sucked at the air, their green eyes glowing in the dark of the wrecker's yard as they stared in hatred.

At first I thought they were going to charge. But no. Something held them back. They seemed frightened of the bus, but not to the point of giving up. Instead of charging they slid and slithered around each other like piles of slime-filled garbage bags. Finally they surrounded the bus. I was trapped.

Why didn't they come for me?

I looked around. The shoe.

Dawn's mother's shoe. She had died in that bus. And I had been there. But I couldn't remember what had happened. I had tried to remember a thousand times. But the memory of it was gone. Knocked out by the crash.

Had Dawn's mum been drunk? Had she crashed the bus on purpose like some people thought but didn't like to say? I had *her* to thank for my limp and my twisted leg. If it wasn't for her I'd have been able to run faster than Dawn. If she hadn't died, Dawn wouldn't be my step-sister. My mum would still be married to Dad. And we all would have been happy. It was all Louise's fault.

The shoe made me angry. It was a rotting reminder of Dawn's mum and how she had crashed the bus. With me in it.

I picked up the worn shoe and held it in front of my eyes.

Outside in the night I heard a huge swooshing noise. Almost as if a hundred mouths had sucked in breath at the same time. It was the slobberers. They were blinking their eyes and sighing.

They didn't seem to like the shoe either.

Without thinking I ran over to the door and threw the shoe out like a hand grenade. 'Cop that,' I yelled.

The shoe bounced right through a bunch of slobberers and landed next to the remains of a clapped-out

Land Rover. The slobberers squealed and wriggled away backwards. I laughed hysterically to myself. They didn't like it. The shoe had them worried.

Except for one little group that had other problems.

They were stretched out in the shadows. Groaning. Almost as if they were sick. The very sound of their wailing sent waves of revulsion through my shaking body.

I looked around the bus. There was no way out. Sunrise was a long way off. And so was Dawn.

If she was still alive.

I was alone. Outside were the slobberers. And inside – terrors as yet unknown.

I slumped down onto the floor and sunk my head into my hands. My cut fingers ached and throbbed. I felt as if I had an awful bout of the flu. The inside of the bus seemed to warp and bend. Strange things were happening. My whole body was racked with wild, uncontrollable shaking.

I turned to my little apple-man for comfort as I had done many times before. The way a child turns to a teddy bear in the darkness of the night.

I stared down at him and tried to focus. My father's last gift. But this time there was no comfort. Was it my eyes, or was my apple-man changing?

Yes, he was changing. Slowly at first so that I

couldn't quite make out what was happening. Then faster.

His face began to squirm and boil. It warped and bubbled and re-formed itself. The eyes became evil slits. Sharp, cruel teeth erupted from its lips. Pointed ears sprouted from the head. The mouth opened and a mocking, blue, forked tongue flickered out.

Oh, horror of horrors. Something else. Worse. Oh, so much worse.

A whining, high-pitched, cackling laugh came from its mouth. Like a tortured chainsaw squeal, the sound filled the air.

The contorted head began to swell, larger and larger, until it was the size of a football. *Whang, sploosh, cackle*. The head exploded and filled the bus with the stench of a thousand farts.

Then there was nothing left except a dry skin which began to smoke and burn.

Oh, no, no, no. I dropped the shredded remains of the apple-man to the floor and screamed.

Was there no end to this nightmare?

Everything was changing. Even in the moonlit shadows I could tell that the bus had more sick secrets to tell. The seats were no longer torn and cracked. And the smashed speedometer now had a sparkling new face. I stared out through the windscreen. The tree that had grown out of the bonnet was still there. But it was smaller. Not broken or pruned. Just smaller.

I stared at it. It was shrinking. Slowly, slowly, slowly, the tree was shrinking.

'It's un-growing,' I gasped to myself.

I heard something above me and looked up. A moth buzzed at enormous speed around my head. So fast that I could hardly see it.

I looked down. Beside me on the floor a tiny lizard scampered quickly away and into a small rust hole. Backwards.

I shook my head in disbelief. 'What the heck is going on?' I yelled.

No one answered. There *was* no one.

On the wall of the bus a patch of rust was disappearing and being replaced by red paint. A faded poster was growing brighter and renewing itself. The photo of a doctor stared down. Underneath in bold letters it said, ARE YOU SICK? WE'RE HERE TO HELP.

I looked along the aisle. There was no one there. No one to help me.

The goat's skeleton still sat in the seat where it had died. But now it was different. Its bones were no longer bleached. And small pieces of dried flesh and skin clung to some of the ribs.

I stared at it with widening eyes. Last time I was there, those bones were as dry and smooth as old wood. I backed away – unable to even scream.

Another foul odour started to fill the air. A disgusting, dead-flesh smell. My eyes watered and my stomach heaved as the revolting smell choked the inside of the bus. I pinched my nose with my fingers and ran to a broken window and started to gulp in fresh air.

I only managed a couple of gasps. The shattered window un-shattered. Pieces of broken glass flew up from the floor and from the ground outside. In an instant the window was whole and re-made. I fell back into a seat and began to scream and scream and scream.

Every cell in my body begged me to leave that bus. That stinking jail. That terrible refuge. Making itself new.

I stared at the goat. I couldn't take my eyes away from the skeleton as flesh slowly re-formed on the bones.

Slobberers. An un-rotting goat. A window re-made. A bus becoming new.

Terrible, terrible, terrible.

But all made small next to the one sight which had burned itself into my frenzied mind. A vision which would remain with me for ever. Like the worm

RORY

spelling *Karl* in my bedroom . . .

The face . . . The wicked face on the apple-man when it exploded . . .

Had been the face of my father.

THREE

Keep a clear head, I told myself as I strode across the wrecker's yard. You need a clear head when you're going to beat a hundred slobberers to death with a steel fence post.

My head wouldn't listen. It kept filling up with Dad. And how I didn't know if I was ever going to see him again.

That thought should have made me even angrier. Even more determined to pulp the slobberers. It didn't. It just made me sadder.

As I got closer to them I felt my anger draining away. My legs started to feel heavy. So did the steel fence post.

Then I realised the dopeyness of what I was trying to do. One kid, forty-eight kilos in her boots. A hundred assorted slobberers, eighteen thousand kilos not including the slime.

How many could I kill before

they sucked out *my* bones?

Fifty?

Twenty-eight?

Three?

And what if Dad *was* still alive? How'd he feel coming along afterwards with the army and finding me tossed onto the roof of the bus, just an empty bag of skin?

Suddenly my whole body started shaking and I wondered if I could make it to the gate before the slobberers attacked.

I looked at them sprawled around the bus in the moonlight. Then I stared. They weren't moving. Not even their eyes. They looked like they were asleep. Why not? I thought. Maggots sleep.

Then I had another thought. What if Rory was in the bus? Cowering in there now, too terrified to come out? Waiting for me to rescue him?

I took a deep breath.

I didn't want him in my life but I couldn't leave him to die.

Perhaps I could make it. Perhaps I could get to the bus if I crept really quietly. Making sure I didn't kick any scrap metal or tread on any tongues.

I gripped my fence post tighter and tried to spot a clear path between the dozing slobberers.

Then I saw it. Lying next to the axle of a wrecked

four-wheel drive. Slobberers all around it. Scuffed and mouldy and dirty but unmistakeable.

Mum's shoe.

My stomach lurched.

The last time I'd seen it, it had been on the bus. Under the driver's seat. Right where she died.

How did it get out here?

The slobberers must have slimed onto the bus and dragged it off, hoping there were human bones in it.

I shuddered at the thought of filthy slobberers squabbling over Mum's shoe. Well, they weren't having it any more. If Dad was dead, it was the last remaining bit of both my parents and it was mine.

Heart pounding, I started picking my way between the slobberers.

Closer.

Closer.

Please, I silently begged the giant grubs. Don't be light sleepers.

Closer.

Closer.

Got it.

I pressed Mum's shoe to my chest and squeezed my neck muscles really hard to stop a sob coming out. It wasn't easy. For a second it was like Mum was there with me but I knew she wasn't and that was almost more than I could bear.

Then I remembered I was surrounded by slobberers.

I pulled myself together. But only for a second. A horrible thought hit me. This was what it must have been like for Rory when the slobberers flooded into the yard. All around him like this. Except worse. Charging at him, slurping, ravenous.

That's when I knew Rory must be dead. I started shaking again and I had to squeeze my neck muscles as hard as I could. I hoped it had been even quicker for Rory than it had been for the dog.

Then I concentrated on getting out of there. The longer I hung around being sad and wobbly, the more chance I'd wake up the slobberers.

Halfway back they woke up anyway. Or at least I thought they had. I caught a glimpse of movement. My heart stopped. Movement all around me. My head spun. Then I realised it wasn't bodies that were moving, it was skin.

While the slobberers slept, their skin was starting to fester and bubble like cream cheese past its use-by date.

I hurried on, trying not to look. What was happening? Perhaps it was just because they were adults. Eileen always complained that she got dry painful skin at night.

I stepped past the last slobberer, hoping desperately it wouldn't wake up and be as grumpy as Eileen was in the mornings.

Then I ran for the gate.

My plan was to get back to town and find a phone and raise the alarm and the armed forces of several nations.

In the middle of Dead Cow Clearing another awful thought hit me. The slobberers on the bridge over the river. What if they weren't all sleeping and having skin problems? What if some were guarding the roads into town?

I decided to go cross-country and head into town through the paddocks behind Agnelli's dairy.

It wasn't easy, going bush at night. In less than an hour I was scratched and sore and exhausted. I wasn't even sure I was going in the right direction. Dad had taught me to use the stars, but now the clouds kept getting in the way.

I hung onto my fence post just in case. At about three a.m. I was glad I had. I'd just painfully unhooked myself from a thorn bush when I saw movement ahead in the gloom.

I froze.

Several slobberer-sized shapes were watching me.

Then a cloud shifted off the moon and I saw it was

only a mob of sheep. They had weird expressions on their faces, just like the one in the wrecker's yard. My neck prickled. Must be an imported breed, I thought, with unusual jaw bones.

'Dunno why you're grinning,' I said loudly. 'You won't find any feed here under the trees.'

The sheep turned and trotted off. Then stopped and looked back at me. Then trotted some more. Then looked back again.

I had the crazy thought that they wanted me to follow them. It was my turn to grin. Dopey sheep. But I didn't grin for long. Suddenly they all came back and surrounded me and several started butting me behind the knees. When I tried to free myself they closed in tighter. Then they started herding me towards an open paddock.

As the shock wore off I tried to stay calm. Relax, my desperately tired brain told my desperately tired body. You're being rescued by a mob of sheep. They're grateful for the considerate way Dad always warms the shears first.

After a fair bit of herding I saw the dark shape of a building and recognised where the sheep had brought me.

The Piggot place. Ernie Piggot had tried to run sheep too far up Bald Mountain and he'd gone broke and got into a big fight with the bank. Eileen had done heaps of courier trips out to him with legal documents before he'd got evicted.

Dad had told me that when Ernie had gone he'd left the phone on with a rude answering-machine message to the bank. When I saw it was his place my heart gave an exhausted thump of joy. 'Thanks, guys,' I said to the sheep.

The door was open. I blundered around in the dark. Finally I found the phone socket.

No phone.

I was too tired to cry. I just lay down on the bare boards with the fence post next to me. I hugged Mum's shoe and thought how normal my life had been until twelve hours ago and how sad and weird and scary it was now.

As I fell asleep I thought I heard a strange sound from outside. No, it couldn't be. Sheep didn't laugh.

FOUR

Dad, Dad, Dad. **Why** did I see your face just before the apple-man exploded? And why was it twisted and horrible and ugly?

'You don't look like that. You don't, you don't, you don't,' I screamed to myself.

I had no time to figure it out. Another horror was about to start. The retreat of the flies.

In they flew. Buzzing in reverse gear. Settling like a black, boiling blanket near the rotting flesh of the goat.

Why was this bus set on rewind? Was it really happening? Or was I mad?

I couldn't tear my eyes away from the goat. Now, where the flies had been there was a mass of pale-coloured things. A moving mass.

My head hurt terribly. I found it hard to focus my eyes. What was going on?

No, no, no, no, no. The pupae were slowly turning back into

maggots. Hungry maggots. Wriggling towards the rotting body of the goat.

At first there were just a few. Then a couple of dozen. Then hundreds. And thousands. And millions. They were centimetres deep crawling right across the floor. Squirming and squiggling by the barrow-load.

As they seethed on the carcass of the goat, it filled with more and more rotting flesh. The maggots were disgorging, not eating their meal – but un-eating it.

I gagged and retched as the foul stench filled the air. I had to get out. I threw up on the wall. Gasping in agony I stumbled to the door.

Suddenly I stopped.

I couldn't leave and face the slobberers. Never. And I couldn't stay either. Think, think, think. I pulled my windcheater over my head and blocked out the ghastly sight of the maggots.

Inside my own little black space I stole a second or two and tried to clear my head. For all I knew the waiting slobberers had killed Dawn. And my mum.

Poor Dawn. She didn't seem so bad now. Not now that she was gone. I would have given anything just to have seen her ugly mug again. She would have been someone to talk to. She was a pain in the bum. But she was human. And she was strong. A little reminder of home.

RORY

Home. It seemed so far away. Normal. Hamburgers. Cereal. My bed. Milk in the fridge. Arguments about photos and Milo tins.

It seemed so wonderful. So unreal. So distant.

The thought of it gave me a speck of courage and I pulled the windcheater down off my head. Through watering eyes I peered at the great carcass. It stank as much as ever but there weren't as many maggots. Shoot. Was this really happening? Each maggot was being replaced by a small, white egg.

The maggots were going back into their eggs.

Bzzzz. Now what? The number of flies was building up. Oh no. A billion buzzing blowflies blackened the air and filled it with an ear-splitting whine. Flying furiously backwards. The parents of the first lot. The ones that laid the eggs. They were coming back for what they had left behind. Each fly stopped for an instant on the pink flesh and took its eggs, one by one, back into its body. The flies were un-laying their eggs.

The stench was bad. I choked and staggered. I covered my mouth and tried not to breathe in the hideous fumes. My head seemed to float in space. My hand throbbed. But I could still work out what was happening.

The bus and everything in it was being made new.

Growing younger. Renewing itself.

The dials. The seats. The dead goat.

They were going back to the way they once were. Before the bus crash.

The goat was now fully fleshed and covered in a white, hairy coat. Flies still buzzed backwards but there were fewer of them. The goat's empty eye sockets seemed to be staring at me. Then, slowly but surely, the sockets began to fill, almost as if some invisible sculptor was re-making them. Dead, black pupils appeared and then the yellowy brown of the eyes.

The smell began to weaken and then it was gone. So were the flies. There was just me and the goat. And my throbbing hand, which was growing more and more painful.

The dead goat seemed to mock me from its seat. I hated that goat. I hated it.

As the hate grew inside me I noticed that a bruise was spreading up my arm. Almost as if the anger was feeding it.

It was a silly thing to do. A stupid, weak thing. But it was all I could think of. I stuck my fingers into the air. 'Nick off,' I yelled.

Oh, why did I say that? Why, why, why? The goat gave a loud bleat, jumped to its feet and ran past me down the aisle backwards. It slipped and skidded and then wriggled bum first through the door, back the way it must have come when it had entered.

I couldn't believe it. The goat was alive.

But I was nearly dead. With fear. I fell back against the seat and stared around the bus. I was alone. Thank goodness for that. My rotting companion had gone.

The inside of the bus stopped warping and bending and grew still. My head began to clear.

Everything in the bus was back to new. The paint-work was fresh. The vinyl seats were shining. The floor was clean. The steering wheel and instrument panel were in perfect condition. The ignition key was in the lock.

The tree that had been growing through the bonnet had disappeared.

The bus was ready to go. And outside the sun beat down from high in the sky.

One lonely fly circled above my head. Forwards. The backward journey was over.

I heard a footfall on the step outside. Someone was there. Someone was coming. My heart leapt in my chest. Thump-fear. Thump-hope. Thump-fear. Thump-hope. The aching bruise washed up and down my arm like a purple wave on a beach.

The driver's door opened and someone stepped in. Was it Dawn? Was it Dad, come to save me? I couldn't see at first in the glare of the midday sun. It was a human. Oh yes, a person, not a slobberer. Someone else to share the terror. Maybe even someone to make it go away.

I peered more closely. The visitor was wearing a uniform. And shoes that I had seen before.

The bright sunlight made the new arrival into a silhouette against the windscreen. Who was it? I watched the shadowy form sit down in the driver's seat. I stared at those familiar shoes as the left foot depressed the clutch. A gloved hand turned the ignition key and the engine sprang to life. The bus began to rock gently as if it was parked at a bus stop waiting for passengers.

Then the driver turned. And smiled.

I didn't return the smile. I screamed.

The driver was Louise. Dawn's dead mother.

FIVE

I dreamed I was asleep on a hard wooden floor and someone was shaking me.

Then I woke up and someone *was* shaking me.

'Dawn,' she was saying. 'What are you doing here? You look terrible.'

I blinked in the daylight. A woman was bending over me. A woman I knew.

'Mum,' I screamed.

I staggered to my feet. My neck and back were so stiff from the floor that I could hardly get my arms up to throw them round her, but I managed.

Then I stopped.

It wasn't Mum, it was Eileen.

My guts dropped with disappointment. The kind of disappointment you feel when you think your mum's come back from the dead and then you find it's just the woman your dad's replaced her with.

'What's going on?' Eileen was saying, concerned. 'Is Rory here?'

I stared at her. She had twigs in her hair, lamb stew on her face, and her arm was in a sling made from Dad's camping shirt.

'Dad,' I gasped. 'Where is he? Is he all right?'

'He's fine,' said Eileen. She sat on the floor with a groan. 'We had an accident yesterday and I was concussed so he went back to town to get help.' She frowned. 'For some reason he didn't come back.'

My heart stopped beating, partly because of what might have happened to Dad, and partly because of what I could see charging through the door behind Eileen.

A sheep.

With a rusty dinner fork in its mouth.

Prongs aimed at Eileen.

I pushed Eileen one way and dived the other. The sheep tried to turn towards Eileen but its hooves couldn't get a grip on the floorboards and it skittered over to the other side of the room. It dropped the fork, sneered at us and ran out the other door.

'What are you doing?' Eileen was shouting. She sat up, holding her hurt arm.

'Sorry,' I said, dazed, not sure if it had really happened. 'A sheep tried to stab you with a fork.' I realised how dopey that sounded. 'It was probably just trying to be playful,' I added uneasily.

Eileen didn't look playful. She took a deep breath. She had the expression she got first thing in the morning if she found there was no coffee.

'Listen,' she growled, standing up. 'I've got a sprained shoulder, badly bruised ribs, I've just spent the night sleeping in a ditch, I walked two hours to use the phone here and it's gone, and I'm not in the mood for stupid games.' She grabbed my arm. 'So why aren't you at home, and where's Rory?'

I gulped. My mouth was dry. How could I tell her? How could I just announce that her son's innards had been sucked out by giant worms and that his skin was probably flapping somewhere in the morning breeze?

I turned away, struggling to find the words and keep the tears in. Then I saw something out of the window. A sheep running across the paddock with an electrical cord in its mouth, dragging a phone and answering machine behind it.

'Look,' I yelled. 'There's the phone.'

We dashed out of the house. The sheep tried to run faster but we soon caught it. As we took the phone the sheep tried to bite us, but we pushed it away. Then we ran back into the house and plugged the phone in.

It didn't work. The whole thing was covered with

teeth marks and the cord was half chewed through.

Eileen swore. I stared at the cord and felt dread seeping through my guts. Eileen turned to me.

'Well?' she said.

I knew I couldn't put off telling her any longer. I tried to prepare her for it by starting at the very beginning. The slobberers in the church. In the stew. On her bike.

'Great,' she exploded. 'That's really going to help my courier deliveries, having my bike at the bottom of a dam.'

I couldn't look her in the eye, so I squinted out the window. Several sheep were struggling across the sunlit front yard, dragging an old garden rake. 'Look,' I whispered in alarm.

'Don't try and change the subject,' snapped Eileen, not taking her eyes off me.

Miserably, I carried on with my story. I told her about finding the car, the boat trip, the airborne slobberers and finally, in a tearful whisper, what had happened at the wrecker's yard.

Eileen listened without saying anything. Then she said a lot.

'I'm disgusted with you, Dawn,' she said angrily. 'Taking my bike and crashing it into a dam is one thing. Coming out with a heap of disgusting and hurtful and ridiculous lies to try and wriggle out of it is ... is ...

I'd have expected more of you than that.'

'It's true,' I sobbed. 'It is.'

She looked at me with narrow eyes for what seemed like ages. 'All right,' she said at last. 'Looks like there's only one way to handle this, young lady. We'd better go to Lumley's wrecker's yard and have a look at these slobberers of yours.'

'That wouldn't be a good idea,' I whispered.

'Oh, yes it would,' she said. 'Come on.' She strode out of the house.

I grabbed Mum's shoe and hugged it to try and make myself feel better. Then I went through the door after Eileen.

She was glaring at me over her shoulder and yelling 'hurry up' and not seeing that she was stepping on a garden rake lying on the overgrown path. The handle flew up, just missed her head and smashed into the wall of an old shed.

My guts tightened. It was the rake the sheep had been dragging.

Before I could say anything, Eileen grabbed me by the arm and yanked me after her in the direction of the wrecker's yard.

'Step it out,' she said. 'We've got a long walk.'

'Eileen,' I pleaded. 'You don't realise how dangerous the slobberers are.'

'Don't worry,' she replied. 'Nothing gets in my road. I'm a courier.'

Okay, I thought bitterly. Have it your way. You're the adult.

She obviously didn't believe a word I'd told her. So I didn't even bother telling her what I'd just seen behind the old shed.

Four grinning sheep sitting on a tractor.

SIX

Dawn's Mum was dead. Yet there she was, sitting in the driver's seat of the bus. Smiling at me. Had she come back to life like the dead goat? Was she a ghost?

There was one thing for sure. Whatever she was I wasn't hanging around to find out. I charged down the aisle of the bus and leapt out after the goat. My feet didn't even touch the steps. I crashed onto the ground and rolled over and over and over. Finally I came to rest next to a pile of old steering wheels in the wrecker's yard.

The sun was starting to peep over the horizon. The first rays of morning scratched their way across the sky. But I had no time for the view. I could think of only one thing. The slobberers.

The slobberers would suck me up for breakfast. I remembered the caretaker's dog and what they had done to him.

34

I wanted to run but I couldn't get up. I was exhausted, weak and alone. This was it. This was the end of my life.

Now that the moment had come I felt calm. My hand and arm stopped aching. The panic fled from me and my thoughts turned to other things. Actually, if the slobberers sucked me up I would be famous. The adults could get my skin and stuff it. Like Phar Lap, the racehorse.

I would be the boy who gave up his life to the slobberers.

I lay there on the ground next to the clapped-out Land Rover and waited for the slimy tongues to come for me.

I waited.

And waited.

Nothing happened.

Nothing at all. I slowly lifted my head and looked around. The wrecked cars littered the yard like ghostly chariots. The bus rusted away and the tree that grew through its bonnet stood still and silent in the morning mist.

The slobberers had gone. Not a sign of them.

Yes. Gone. My heart leapt and I felt my energy return. I was safe. It was all over.

But where were they? An image of Dawn fleeing

through the night filled my mind. Had the slobberers gone after her? Were they hunting her like a pack of hungry seals?

I suddenly felt sad. I had no right to be safe while she was in danger. Okay, she was a pain. But she didn't deserve to die like that. Sucked out into an ugly mat. Even a step-sister didn't deserve to end up like that.

My arm felt warm and the ache fell away completely. Almost as if my thoughts were healing it. But the angry purple bruise was still there.

I stared at the rusting bus. The rusting bus? A few minutes ago it had been covered in fresh paint. Its engine had been running. But now it just sat there on its flat tyres. Battered and broken and wrecked. The motor looked as if it hadn't run for years.

And wait a minute. When I was in the bus the sun outside had been high in the sky. And now it was only just peeping over the hills.

What was going on? The sun can't go backwards. A bus can't be made new again. My fingers began to throb and the wound started to weep.

I wanted to run home. Every nerve in my body was stretched to breaking point. I looked at the bus. What was that on the step? It couldn't be. But it was. The apple-man.

I tried to swallow but my tongue was dry with fear. The apple-man's face had become the face of my father. Horrible and distorted. Then it had exploded. And yet here it was, whole and intact.

Slowly and in a daze I walked back to the bus. I picked up the apple-man and with knocking knees climbed the steps and looked inside. The goat's skeleton sat there, its dry white bones glowing in the red rays of dawn. Dust covered the seats and spider webs barred the broken windows.

There were no maggots. No flies. There was no Louise. Just an empty, decaying cabin of dreams.

Was it a dream? Never.

Nightmare? Maybe.

Had any of this happened at all?

A thought crept into my mind. If it hadn't been a nightmare or a dream what was it? Maybe I was ill. My nervous system might be collapsing. All the pressures of Dad going out of my life and Dawn coming into it could be weakening my brain. Making me see things. Was my step-sister driving me crazy?

I sat there on the steps of the bus in misery.

Think, think, think. Some things might only be happening inside my head. I hit my forehead with my good hand and tried to get my brain back into gear.

Go back over it all. Pick out the bits that are real

and the bits that aren't.

Louise — starting up the bus. Dead people don't drive. Maybe she didn't die after all.

The apple-man. Did it explode? No. Because it was still in one piece in my hands.

The shoe. Was there a shoe? I looked around near the Land Rover. No sign of it. There was some dried-up blobs of cow dung on the ground but no shoe. No, there couldn't have been a shoe.

The slobberers. Not one in sight. They must have just been in my head, my insane mind.

Dawn. Was there any such person as big bad Dawn? Yes, because she had been at my school since the bubs' class. But her mother mustn't have died. Fantastic. Maybe Dawn's dad Jack wasn't married to my mum. Maybe we were all together still. Me and Mum and Dad. In our old house. Our real house. Yes, yes, yes. Oh, someone wake me up. Or take me home.

I looked down at the apple-man and my joy fled. Dad had sent me that apple-man after the bust-up with Mum. Louise *had* died. The step-marriage *had* happened. Dawn *was* my step-sister.

I wandered slowly around the wrecker's yard trying to work out what was real and what wasn't.

The caretaker. He would help me. I made my way over to his little hut and looked inside. His reading lamp was still on but the room was empty. A dog chain and a bowl of dog food lay on the floor. There was no sign of the dog. I felt so lonely and scared.

And my hand had started to hurt again.

My hand. I had cut it climbing over the fence. And . . . A shudder ran down my spine. Slobberers had licked my fingers and sucked the blood. Hadn't they? I wasn't sure about anything any more.

I limped over to the fence. Yes, there were traces of blood on the rusting metal.

The climb over the fence had taken place all right. But the bit in the bus hadn't. Half of the mad things had happened. And half hadn't. Maybe I was only half mad.

The marriage was real. The apple-man was real. And Dawn was real. The blood on the fence was real. But had slobberers licked it or were they invented by my warped mind?

I decided to leave the wrecker's yard for good. It was time to go home. It was time to get help. I needed a shrink to put me on the right track.

As I moved something caught my eye. A dark shadow on the ground. That sent me screaming down the road.

It was the flat, empty body of the caretaker's dog.

SEVEN

I **had something on** my mind all the way back to the wrecker's yard.

Sheep.

I knew sheep pretty well, and I'd never seen them attack a person before. Not with a garden rake. Definitely not with a table fork.

What's going on? I wondered anxiously as I plodded along behind Eileen.

Were the sheep just grouchy because Ernie Piggot had upped and gone and left them?

Or were they out to get us like the slobberers?

A shiver of fear ran through me. I thought about the sheep on the tractor. Could sheep get a tractor

started? I told myself to stop being dopey.

Then I realised Eileen had turned and was yelling at me. 'Stop dragging your feet,' she snapped. 'I want to get this charade over with. The sooner we knock this giant worm nonsense on the head, the sooner I can find out what's going on.'

She grabbed me by the arm and I had to trot to keep up with her. Then we both crashed to the ground.

There was a length of fencing wire stretched across the dirt track. As I tripped and fell forward I noticed something glinting in the dust. When my head cleared after the impact I saw what it was.

Glass. Jagged pieces of brown glass. Luckily I hadn't landed on any of them. Neither had Eileen. Having her arm in a sling had made her fall to one side. She lay on the grass verge, swearing.

Then I recognised a torn label on one of the pieces of glass. Sheep dip. We'd been tripped up so we'd cut ourselves on broken sheep-dip bottles.

I sat up in a panic and looked around. Sheep were watching us from each side of the track. I was just in time to see one of them open its mouth and drop an end of the fencing wire.

'Eileen.' My voice was a whisper. 'These sheep are out to get us.'

The sheep grinned menacingly.

'Bulldust,' yelled Eileen, struggling to her feet. She dragged me up. 'It's just kids playing stupid tricks, and if I catch them they'll suffer almost as much as you're going to. Now come on.'

She dragged me along the track. I glanced nervously over my shoulder. The sheep had gone. I was almost disappointed. If they whacked Eileen round the head with a fence post, then she'd know I wasn't a liar.

You'll see, I thought helplessly. When we get to the wrecker's yard and a hundred slobberers suck your innards out, then you'll see I was telling the truth.

At that moment I remembered I'd left my fence post back at Ernie Piggot's house. I tried to turn back, but Eileen's grip was unbreakable.

At least I had Mum's shoe inside my shirt.

I held it tight through the cloth. It made me feel better even though it wasn't much good as a weapon.

We were close to the wrecker's yard. I strained my ear for sounds of slobberers. My heart was pounding so loudly I couldn't hear much. Just some birds screeching and Eileen muttering about kids and their warped minds.

At the gate I stopped. 'Let's go to the police,' I pleaded. 'They can come and take photos of the slobberers and you can see those.'

Eileen looked at me grimly. 'If we're going to be a family, Dawn, we've got to start being honest with each other.'

She dragged me through the gate.

'No,' I yelled desperately. 'We don't stand a chance. They haven't eaten for hours. We'll be – '

I stopped and stared. The yard was empty. There wasn't a slobberer to be seen.

I tore my arm free and ran around the piles of scrap and the bus and the four-wheel drive and the big wrecker's crane, looking wildly.

Nothing.

'Okay, young lady,' yelled Eileen. 'Come here and start talking.'

I ignored her. I ran back to the bus and peered in, not caring if a tidal wave of slobberers poured out. At least then she'd know.

The bus was empty. Just the torn seats and the smashed speedometer and the goat's skeleton.

'Dawn,' roared Eileen.

Slowly I turned to face a life of not being believed and possibly being accused of killing and eating Rory.

Then I noticed something. On the ground. Big patches of what looked like cow poo. Dry and cracked. But not crumbly like cow poo. Hard like dried leather. When I kicked one I hurt my foot.

Of course. I remembered the slobberers' festering skins. They must have been dying. But what could have made them decompose so fast?

My thoughts were interrupted by Eileen grabbing me.

'I said,' she hissed, 'start talking.'

'They've died and shrivelled up,' I explained desperately. 'Look, you can see where they were. There and there and there and ...'

'Cow dung,' said Eileen icily. 'It's dried cow dung, Dawn. Just like you're feeding me. Now tell me what's going on. Where's Rory?'

As I blinked back tears of rage and frustration, I was tempted to just make something up. 'He's run away from home because you're such a pain', something like that. But I knew Mum wouldn't have approved. She was a stickler for the truth. Even if it meant admitting she was five minutes late with the school bus because she'd got one of her uniform buttons jammed in my high chair.

'There's something weird and scary going on,' I said to Eileen. 'Maggots turning into bone-sucking monsters and sheep behaving in a very unfriendly manner. I don't know why and I don't know how, but it's happening.'

Eileen looked like she was going to explode.

She didn't. 'I shouldn't blame you,' she said, taking a deep breath, 'Not when your mother had so much trouble telling the truth.'

I felt like *I* was going to explode.

Before I could, I heard a loud creak above us. And a whoosh. I looked up. Swinging towards us was the big metal ball hanging from the end of the wrecker's crane.

Except it wasn't a ball of metal, it was a ball of sheep. About six of them, all with evil grins, clinging to the end of the chain.

I couldn't move. I stared horrified as the sheep hurtled towards us. Then I noticed something even worse. The sheep were glinting in the sun. Their wool wasn't soft and fluffy any more, it was hard and metallic.

Steel wool.

EIGHT

I ran screaming down the country road away from the remains of the dog. The glow of dawn and the morning mist meant nothing. My mind was a whirlpool of doubt, fear and horror. Was I mad? Did a goat's skeleton really come to life on that bus? Was Dawn's dead mother really there?

The whole thing was crazy, crazy, crazy. Even now slobberers could be waiting for me in the trees beside the road. Waiting to pounce and suck.

My bad leg ached. And my hand and arm were inflamed again. The purple bruise had spread. Pain filled my whole arm and part of my chest. Was my arm infected? The slobberers had licked me. Did I have

some new illness? Slobberers' disease. Maybe I was dying.

I ran until I could run no further. I fell down exhausted in the middle of the road next to a slimy pond.

Eventually I got my breath

back and sat up. I looked around me. All seemed quiet in the early morning light.

I still clutched the apple-man. I stared down at him. He was a bit grimy so I wiped him on my sleeve. I loved the apple-man. He might have been the home of the slobberers. He might or might not have exploded on the bus. But he was still a gift from my Dad. And even though he was an ugly little doll made out of a dried-up apple I was not going to part with him.

I think I knew, deep down inside me. Even way back then, at the beginning of it all. That the apple-man held the answers to all the questions I was too frightened to ask.

My feet stirred up the dust on the road as I slowly headed for home. Home? It wasn't really my place. Dawn's dad owned the house. And Dawn thought she owned it too. And Gramps, even though he was a nice guy and harmless, wasn't really *my* Gramps. Okay, Mum lived there now. But she always seemed to stick up for Dawn. Like that first time me and Mum went over to their place.

I don't know what all the fuss was about. Just because I made a double slingshot out of Dawn's bra. It could fire two tennis balls at once. Right over the house.

'Golf balls,' I told her. 'One on each side. That's all it would hold.'

Okay, so I lied a bit. And I ruined the bra. But Mum shouldn't have grounded me. Not her own son. Not her own flesh and blood.

I felt hurt. And angry. Really angry. And as I trudged along the road my arm hurt more and more. It was so painful that tears pricked behind my eyelids.

If only Dad were there. He would know what to do. He would know whether I was insane or not. He would stick up for me. He would help.

I looked down at the little apple-man with a bit of a smile and continued to force my aching legs towards the house. 'I'll show them,' I thought. 'You can't treat me like that.'

My arm and chest throbbed more and more. My bad leg ached. I had to rest again. I sank down on a log, exhausted, and closed my eyes.

Something cold and wet moved across my hand. What, what, what? A slobberer's tongue? I was too scared to move. Too scared to open my eyes. But I had to.

Two eyes blinked back at me. Not a slobberer. Only a frog.

I laughed with relief and picked him up gently. 'Hello, little fella,' I said.

The frog shot out his tiny tongue and tickled my cut hand. I could feel the small wet flick of it on the seeping scab of my wound. Suddenly the frog's eyes rolled back in his head and then quivered back into view. Like the symbols on a poker machine when you hit the jackpot.

The frog sat shivering on my palm. Why was it shivering? Frogs don't get cold, do they? Maybe it was scared. Like me.

Then the frog crouched. For a second it was like a coiled spring. Then its eyes rolled, and pow. It shot up into the sky with an enormous leap. Talk about the cow jumping over the moon. It disappeared over the top of the trees. *Splash.* It must have landed back in the pond.

What a jump. Incredible. I had never seen anything like it.

My mind started to tick over. The frog licking me. It reminded me of something. Something similar. What was it?

Then it clicked. The slobberers had licked my bleeding hand. And then there was the sheep. On the step of the bus, I had stuck my cut finger into the sheep's nostril.

Maybe there was some sort of disease going around. Maybe we were infecting each other. Like the Black Death. I needed help. I had to get home.

I staggered on down the road. On and on. It seemed

such a long way home. Finally I reached the bridge. Not far now. I stopped and listened to the water gurgling below. And heard something else. Behind me in the bushes.

Plip, plop, plip, plop. Like tiny spoonfuls of jelly falling onto the road. Dozens of them. No, hundreds. *Plip, plop, plip, plop, plip, plop.* No, thousands. As if an unseen hand was throwing stones into the air.

There. Stretched across the road. Little green lumps with small blinking eyes. Suddenly they lifted into the air like a swarm of grasshoppers. Up, up, up, up. Way above the treetops. They stopped, paused in mid flight and began to fall. A hailstorm of frogs in the forest.

Whoosh, they landed together. As one. The sound reminded me of a huge bucket of water sloshing on the road. A million frogs, all landing at once.

They blinked at me. Unfriendly. My legs felt so weak I could hardly stand. But somehow I managed to back away from them across the bridge. Not for one second did I take my eyes off the fearful plague.

The frogs, as one, crouched down and then sprang. Way, way, over my head. Right across the river in one – no, not one. But one million identical giant leaps. They sloshed down onto the road and jumped again. And again.

The shower of frogs disappeared into the distance along the dusty road.

Towards our house.

I stumbled after them as fast as I could go. I was nearly there. Home at last. Suddenly it all seemed silly. A nightmare. Unreal. There were no frogs. It was all a mistake. All my tiredness fell away. Even my arm didn't hurt quite as much as I trudged the last few steps up to the gate. Now I could get adult help. They could take over.

Slobberers, a skeleton goat, Dawn's mother back from the dead, an exploding apple-man and frogs that can jump trees. They were all just in my head. Part of my sickness. None of that would matter any more.

A shadowy figure moved in the kitchen window. Mum? Maybe Mum was there by now. And Jack. Oh, I hoped so much that they were. I let out a sob and opened the gate.

A thunderous roar filled the air. It was almost as if the movement of the gate had been a signal for it to start. I clapped my hands over my ears and started running for the front door. What *was* that noise? So loud.

It was an ordinary old noise made bigger. A noise from a peaceful morning in the country. But amplified like a rock band out of control.

RORY

Frogs. A billion frogs croaking together. I couldn't see them but there was no doubt that they were there. Hiding in the trees that surrounded the house.

NINE

'**Look out**,' **I screamed** at Eileen.

She just stood there, in shock, staring.

I didn't blame her. Most people, if they had a choice between paying attention to a step-daughter screaming at them or to six sheep hurtling towards them on a wrecker's ball, would choose the sheep.

Specially if the sheep had razor-sharp steel wool.

I grabbed Eileen's sling and dragged her out of the way. The ball of sheep whooshed past, scowling. I thought how many layers of skin their wool would rip off us if it touched us. Suddenly my legs were pumping.

'Over here,' I yelled at Eileen as I ran towards the bus. I looked back. Eileen was still rooted to the spot, staring at the sheep, stunned. The sheep landed on the roof of the care-taker's office. One lost its grip on the ball and slid across the roof in a spray of rust and metal shavings. The others launched themselves at Eileen again.

I found I was rooted to the spot too. For a fleeting second all I could think about was that Eileen believed the evil gossip about Mum being a liar and the bus crash being Mum's fault. For a fleeting second I almost wanted the sheep to get her. Then I remembered Dad loved her, so I sprinted over and pulled her out of the way again.

'This can't be happening,' she croaked as the sheep whizzed past her head.

'If you think *this* is scary,' I muttered grimly, 'you should have seen what the slobberers did to the dog.' I remembered they'd probably done it to her son too, so I changed the subject. 'We'll be safer in the bus,' I said.

It was too late. The sheep were on the roof of the crane cab preparing for another swing. I looked wildly around. Near us was a pile of scrap. I grabbed Eileen and we tried to squeeze in between a stack of flattened cars and a big old industrial fridge. There wasn't room.

I looked frantically up at the sheep. All six pairs of bloodshot eyes were fixed on Eileen.

That's when I realised the sheep weren't interested in me. They wanted my step-mother.

I pulled Eileen out of the cubbyhole and stood her next to the fridge, directly in the path of the swooping sheep. 'It's you they're after,' I explained, then I squeezed in alongside the fridge.

Eileen didn't move. She must still have been in shock. The sheep hurtled towards her. Just before the ball of sheep gave her the worst skin problem of her life, I flung open the fridge door. The ball, and the sheep, slammed into it.

After the dust had settled, and my heart had dropped back down into my chest, I checked none of the sheep on the ground were moving. Then I checked Eileen.

'Are you okay?' I asked.

She nodded, shaking. I was shaking too. If I'd been any later opening that fridge door, Dad would have killed me.

'We've got to get back to town,' I said, 'and find Dad and tell the cops what's going on. They'll believe it coming from you.'

Eileen nodded again. She didn't look as though *she'd* believe it coming from her.

We set off back to town on foot, me keeping a nervous eye out for sheep. Eileen didn't say anything for about ten minutes. I understood. My nerves were a mess too. Plus adults took longer to adjust. It was the same with Dad when I dyed my hair green.

As we plodded along the dusty road, I tried not to worry about Dad. It was hard with his shirt wrapped round Eileen's arm and my dazed brain so full of scary questions.

Was the whole world being attacked by giant worms and killer sheep? Or was it just us?

If it was just us, why?

Suddenly Eileen started talking. 'Those slitherers or blubberers or whatever you called them. Where did they come from?'

I told her how they'd started out as normal grubs in the souvenir apple-man Rory's dad had sent him.

Eileen stopped walking and her face went even grimmer than the time I dried my hair on her white towel. The time I discovered the dye wasn't permanent.

She started pacing around and muttering to herself, the way adults do when they're wrestling with a really difficult thought.

'He wouldn't,' she said. 'Surely not. No, I'm being stupid.'

'What?' I said.

Eileen stared at me as if she'd forgotten I was there. 'Rory's father,' she said quietly. 'I've been worried he might try and pull a stunt when he heard I was getting married again. Try and get Rory away from me. But this . . .' She winced and shook her head as if the thought was too big even for someone like her who'd finished year twelve.

I stared at her. What did she mean? That Rory's father was a giant worm? Or a vicious sheep? That was dopey. But hang on, how did I know it was? I didn't know anything about Rory's father, except that he'd nicked off when Rory was five. Rory never wanted to talk about him. He could be a Martian for all I knew. Or a really skilful sheep trainer.

Suddenly the stress of the last day and a half got to me. Something snapped in my head and my brain went woolly with rage. It wasn't fair. Me and Dad had been happy till he'd got involved with Eileen and Rory and their psycho family.

'Why me?' I screamed. 'I'm sick of this.'

Eileen didn't reply. She was straining to hear something. Then I heard it too. It sounded like a tractor, accelerating towards us at speed.

I turned and couldn't believe what I was seeing. Roaring towards us round a bend in the road was Ernie Piggot's tractor. Riding it were four sheep. One had its front legs on the steering wheel. One was sitting on the accelerator pedal. One had the gearstick in its mouth.

The fourth was sprawled on the engine cover. Jutting out from under its tummy, like a knight's lance, was my steel fence post.

Its jagged point was speeding towards us.

DAWN

We screamed and ran. Ahead I spotted a small shack that had once been a roadside fruit stall. Juicy Melons said the sign. Behind us I could hear the tractor getting closer.

We dived in and slammed the ricketty door. The shack shuddered and dust and splinters showered down on us. Then I realised Mum's shoe wasn't inside my shirt. Desperately I peered through a crack in the flimsy wall. There was the shoe, on the road outside. And there, thundering towards us like angry knights in steel-wool armour, were the sheep.

I couldn't look. I buried my face in Eileen's sling, and as we waited for the walls to cave in I realised this was the first time I'd ever hugged my step-mother.

TEN

Home. Safe at last, I hoped.

I lurched down the garden path and crashed through the front door. It hadn't even been locked but I soon took care of that.

'Rory,' croaked a friendly voice.

It wasn't Mum's voice but any human voice would have been friendly at that moment. Especially an adult voice.

'Gramps,' I yelled.

Although he wasn't really my Gramps I was starting to feel as if he was. I ran across the room and threw myself into his arms. I tried really hard not to cry but I was so upset that I couldn't say anything for a second or two.

'I was worried about you,' said Gramps. 'Out there all night in this thunderstorm.'

I fought for breath, trying to control the sobs that were trying to escape. I ran and

peered out of the window. 'That's not thunder,' I said. 'It's frogs.'

Outside, the racket was so loud that it almost drowned us out.

'Frogs?' he said. 'Frogs didn't sound like that when I was a boy.' He looked sad. 'But then nothing seems the same any more, does it? I'll make you a nice cup of tea. You look terrible. Then you can tell me where Dawn is. And what's going on.'

'I don't want tea,' I yelled. 'Those frogs are dangerous. I think they're after me. We have to board up the windows. We have to keep them out.'

Gramps ambled over to the stove and put on the kettle. The roar of the frogs suddenly stopped. All was silent outside. But I wasn't fooled. Not after everything that had happened. Anything was possible. The frogs were up to something. I just knew it.

'The thunder has stopped,' said Gramps. 'Now you just settle down and tell me all about it. I won't hear another word until you've got some tea into you.'

Gramps picked up two shoes from beside the door and put some sugar and milk into them. Then he poured the boiling tea into them and handed one to me. He started to sip his tea from the shoe.

'Hey,' I yelled. 'What are you doing? You don't drink tea from a shoe.'

This terrible nightmare was going on and on and on. Surely there was no other weird thing left to happen.

Gramps looked at his shoe of tea and his eyes started to brim with tears. 'You don't, do you,' he said. 'You put feet into shoes. And . . . tea into cups.'

He stood up and fetched two clean cups and poured us some more tea.

'What's wrong with you, Gramps?' I asked gently. 'Yesterday you put a drill in the freezer.'

He just sat there and blinked at me for a bit. I could tell that he was trying to make up his mind whether or not to tell me.

'I'm sick,' he said.

'So am I,' I yelled. 'So am I. We've got the same thing.' I held out my purple arm and waved it in front of his face. 'I got licked by, by, by . . . slobberers. I keep seeing things. Exploding apple-men and, and . . . and a goat came to life. And millions of frogs are – '

'No,' said Gramps. 'We haven't got the same thing. What I've got. You only get it when you're old.'

'Did the slobberers lick you? Did they? Did they?'

He shook his head. 'No,' he said. 'In my day there was no such thing as slobberers. At least I don't think there was.' He scratched his head. I could tell he was trying very hard to think straight. To remember something. 'We had cobblers, though,' he said. 'Yes. They made these.' He held up a cup.

I started to feel really sad. Cobblers made shoes, not cups. 'How did you catch your disease?' I asked slowly.

'No one knows,' said Gramps. 'Some people say that you get it from cooking with aluminium saucepans. But no one really knows.'

I suddenly stopped feeling sorry for myself. Okay, I was seeing things that weren't there. But somehow it was different with Gramps. It was as if he was wearing out. Like an old car or a shoe.

'What's your disease called?' I asked in a whisper.

'I've forgotten,' he said. 'I keep forgetting things. Did I really put a drill in the freezer? I've never been that bad before.'

I didn't know whether or not to tell the truth. In the end I said, 'Don't worry about it. It was only an old drill. No one wanted it.'

His eyes filled with tears and he just sat there. I must have said the wrong thing.

Gramps put a hand on my shoulder. 'Your mum thought I was still well enough to look after you,' he said. 'But soon you'll be looking after me.'

At that very moment the frogs started up their roaring croaks.

I backed away from the windows. *Splat, splot, splitter,*

splatter. The frogs started throwing themselves against the glass.

'It's raining cats and dogs,' yelled Gramps.

'No,' I shrieked. 'Frogs.'

The sound grew louder and louder. Every window was under attack. The frogs were hurling themselves against the house like bullets from a machine gun. In broad daylight they were mounting a crazy attack. Limp, stunned bodies mounded up like green snow on the window sills. The glass above shivered under the blows.

But the windows were strong. And they held. Gramps sat down and shook his head. 'I know this isn't happening,' he said.

Suddenly everything fell silent.

The frogs had fallen back across the lawn. Their first attack had failed and now they were planning something else. Those that weren't dead.

The frogs were getting into a line. It was a terrifying sight. Intelligent frogs. They looked like people queuing up at a bus stop. Except that the line was too long. It wound across the lawn and out of the gate. It stretched down the dusty road and into the forest. I could see it winding over the hill way in the distance on the other side of the trees. Thousands and thousands of little green frogs. Waiting their turn.

What were they up to?

What was their plan?

What did they want?

At the head of the line one large frog stood facing the others. Like a general reviewing his troops.

What were they lining up for? Lunch?

Yes.

The frog at the front – the general – opened his mouth.

And the first frog in the line jumped into it. The general gave a gulp and the poor little creature was gone. The frog general opened his mouth again and the next little victim jumped straight in. The general chewed a couple of times and swallowed. Then he croaked and stretched open his jaws. The next frog obeyed orders. In it went.

One by one the queuing frogs jumped into the gaping mouth. The general munched and crunched. He burped and slurped. And the line shuffled forward. Each little leaper moving anxiously on, impatient to be eaten.

Faster and faster the meal progressed. In they went. Hopping to their doom. Kamikaze frogs. At this rate they would be gone in no time.

And with each swallow, I noticed something happening to the frog general. Something that made the hair stand up on the back of my head.

He was already the size of a dog. Swelling with each swallow like a monstrous balloon. Soon the tiny frogs would not be enough to satisfy him.

He turned his eyes greedily towards us and a loud croak belched out of his mouth.

'Meat,' I said. 'He wants meat.'

Gramps ran to the fridge and threw open the door. He started to chuckle. 'I ate the last sausage yesterday,' he yelled. 'There's not a bit of meat in the house.'

I stared at Gramps' skinny legs.

'Yes there is,' I said.

To be continued in ...

③ Croaked

PAUL JENNINGS and MORRIS GLEITZMAN

Wicked!

3 Croaked

No.3 IN A SIX-PART STORY ONLY £1

Read this excerpt from the next exciting instalment in the *Wicked!* serial

My new house had never seemed less like home.

Gramps and I stared out of the kitchen window. The plague of frogs was still there.

The frog general ate his little soldiers one at a time. He chewed and chomped and sucked and swallowed. And with each mouthful he grew bigger.

The line of frogs shuffled forward like troops waiting for the firing squad. They jumped into his gaping gob without complaint. Without protest. They were sacrificing themselves. But for what?

The frog general was as big as a dog and still growing. The smaller frogs had failed in their attempt to get into the house. So now they were joining forces.

Making one big frog. That could . . . could . . .

Break down the door.

This was crazy. Crazy, crazy, crazy. The frogs could have attacked me on the road. But they had gone right past. Jumped over my head. So who were they after?

It could only be one person. Gramps.

'We have to stop that frog,' I said in a trembling voice.

'Rory,' said Gramps, 'did you know I was a Rat?'

Oh no. He was rambling again. Out of his mind. Now he thought he was a rat.

'The Rats of Tobruk,' he said proudly. 'In the war. We held Rommel off for months. I was in the Tank Corps.'

I tried not to get upset by Gramps' nonsense. The frog general had grown to the size of a sheep. And the line of frogs was leaping faster and faster into his gaping mouth. They reminded me of bullets being loaded into the breech of a gun.

'I wouldn't mind a tank right now,' I said to Gramps. 'We could blow the frog general away.'

Gramps began to chuckle. 'I've got one,' he said. 'I've got a tank. Out the back.'

Oh, it made me sad. It really did. Poor old Gramps.

I had been seeing a few things myself lately. But that was because the slobberers had licked my cut hand.

The infection had spread right up my arm and onto my chest. Sometimes it made my head spin and sent me crazy. I saw things that weren't there.

But Gramps had some other problem. He was off the planet all the time. I never knew what he was going to do next. Not that it made any difference to how I felt. I really liked him. He was a great guy. He was Dawn's gramps, not mine. But he and I were growing close. In the heat of battle. Comrades in arms.

My thoughts turned to Dawn. She was really gutsy. Big, strong and bold. And dead? Oh, I hoped not. I would have given anything to see her walk through that door. I started to feel really mean for calling her big bad Dawn. After all, the step-family was just as bad for her as it was for me.

'This'll fix him,' said Gramps.

I looked up and saw Gramps holding a large sack of salt.

'Frogs and snails and things don't like salt.' He started to laugh and chuckle like a mad man. 'We'll lob it into his gob.'

ThE AUtHoRs

Morris Gleitzman and Paul Jennings are Australia's most popular writers for children. They are also very good friends.

Now, for the first time, they are writing together. Twice as weird, twice as funny, twice as spooky, twice as mind-blowing. If you loved their books before, you'll love *Wicked!* **twice as much.**

There's never been anything like it.

**MorRiS
GleiTZmaN**

Before I started writing with Paul
Jennings I thought my books were
pretty scary.

In *Two Weeks with the Queen* I let a
kid climb the wall of Buckingham
Palace really late at night. In *Misery
Guts* I put a kid in the middle of a
cyclone without warm underwear. In
Blabber Mouth I even made a kid
stuff a live frog into another kid's
mouth.

I thought I was pretty tough. Then I
met Paul. Now I'm writing about
giant bone-sucking worms and killer
sheep.

Help!

PaUL JeNniNGs

I always find it hard to think of titles
for my books. I couldn't think what
to call my first one. Then my daughter
Lyndu heard that school had been
cancelled. '*Unreal!*' she said.

For this series Morris and I suggested
lots of titles. But it wasn't until I
heard my daughter Gemma say,
'Nicole has a *wicked* haircut,' that we
knew we had the best one.

Morris came up with *Battering Rams*
for this book. It's great, but it beats
me how he thought of it. Hang on ...
'Beats Me' isn't bad either ...

The serial continues in ...

④ Dead Ringer

It wasn't a finger. It was a sucker. Or a root. It wormed its way up the little cup Gramps had put his false teeth into, and started drinking the water.

Gramps snored. The root crept towards him. Was it going to put its terrible finger into his ear? Or his mouth? Was it going to drink HIM?

The serial continues in ...

⑤ The Creeper

There was an explosion of flame and a loud whoosh. A blue and yellow fireball hurtled away from us along the road. We stood and watched it, open-mouthed, until it had disappeared over the horizon.

Even when the fireball had gone we still stood staring, because what it had left behind was so incredible. The entire root, kilometres of it, was writhing and twisting in flames.

The serial concludes in ...

⑥ Till Death Us Do Part

I heard a faint, high-pitched rasping.

It was Rory. He was barely breathing. He stared up at me with dull eyes. The colour and life were draining out of his poor, suffering face.

There was nothing I could do.